# BEST FRINTS at SKROOL

Antoinette Portis

A NEAL PORTER BLOOK

**ROARING BROOK PRESS**

NEW YORK

Copyright © 2018 by Antoinette Portis
A Neal Porter Book
Published by Roaring Book Press
Roaring Brook Press is a divisionof Holtzbrinck Publishing Holdings Limited Partnership
175 Fifth Avenue, New York, NY 10010
The art for this book was created using pencil, charcoal, and a Cintiq drawing tablet.
mackids.com

Library of Congress Control Number: 2017957289
ISBN 978-1-62672-871-4

Our books may be purchased in bulk for promotional, educational, or business use.
Please contact your local bookseller or the Macmillan Corporate and Premium
Sales Department at (800) 221-7945 ext. 5442 or by email at
MacmillanSpecialMarkets@macmillan.com

First edition, 2018
Printed in China by Toppan Leefung Printing Ltd., Dongguan City, Guangdong Province
10 9 8 7 6 5 4 3 2 1

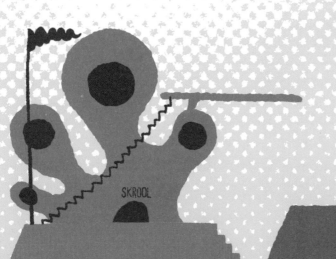

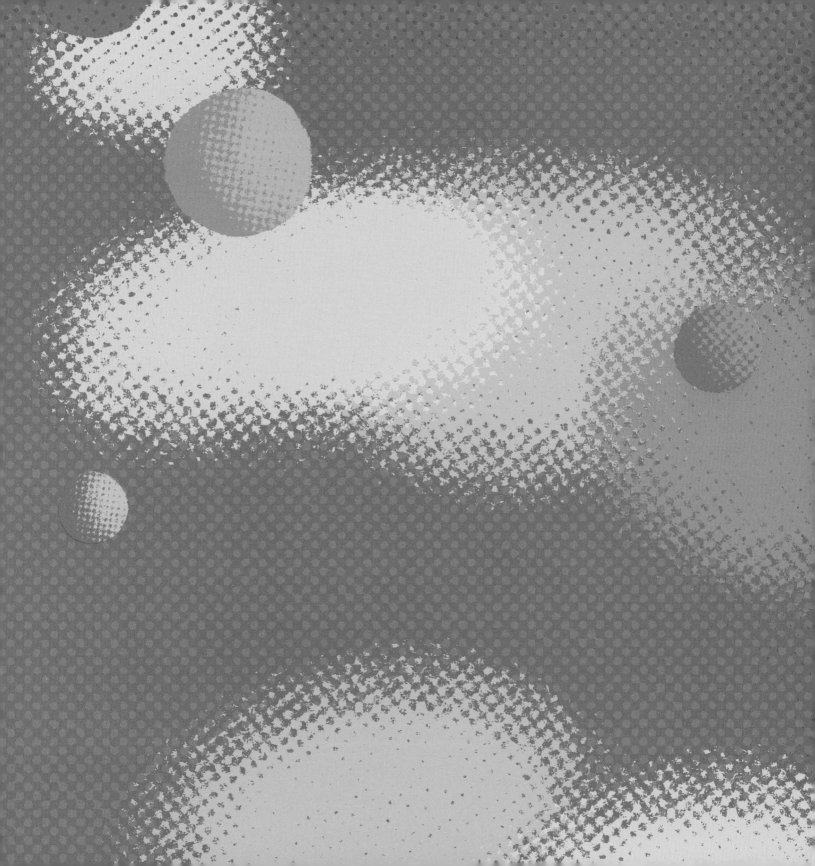

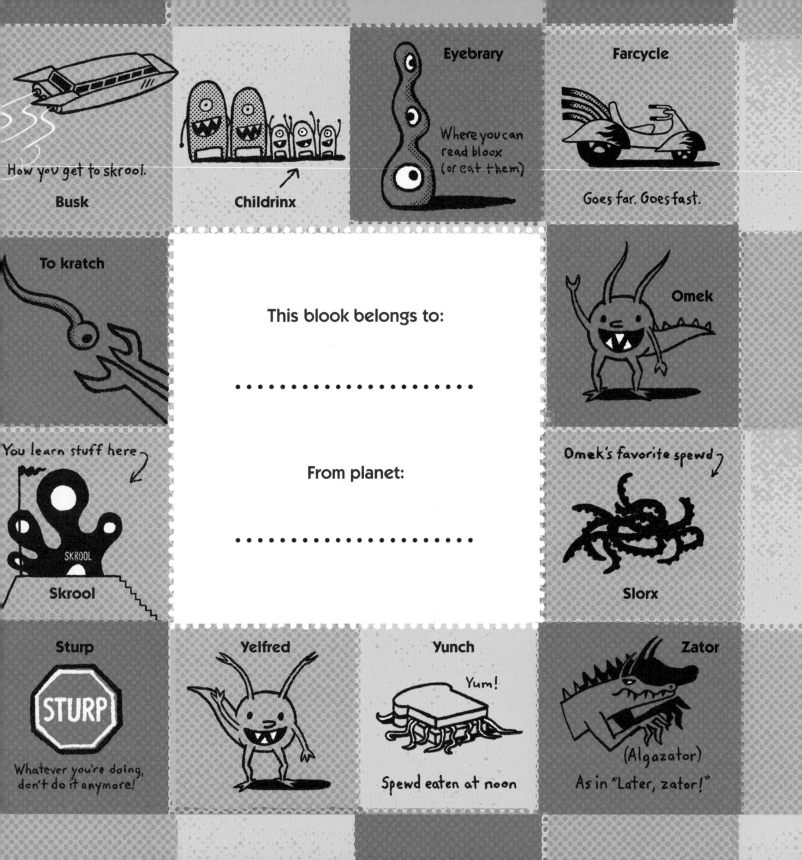

**Busk**
How you get to skrool.

**Childrinx**

**Eyebrary**
Where you can read bloox (or eat them)

**Farcycle**
Goes far. Goes fast.

**To kratch**

This blook belongs to:

. . . . . . . . . . . . . . . . . . . . .

From planet:

. . . . . . . . . . . . . . . . . . . . .

**Omek**

**Skrool**
You learn stuff here
SKROOL

**Slorx**
Omek's favorite spewd

**Sturp**
STURP
Whatever you're doing, don't do it anymore!

**Yelfred**

**Yunch**
Yum!
Spewd eaten at noon

**Zator**
(Algazator)
As in "Later, zator!"

On planet Boborp, childrinx go to skrool,
just like here on planet Earth.

SKROOL

Omek and Yelfred ride the skrool busk.

Unless they're late . . . which is always.

When the bell BLANGS the stroodents sit quietly.

They learn to listen
when their skreecher spleeks . . .

and to keep their tentacles to themselves.

Some stroodents read bloox.

Others eat them.

At recess, childrinx make new frints.

On Boborp, sometimes frints use their words
in ways that aren't so frintly.

(Not like here on planet Earth.)

"Too bad, Omek, no room for you.
Threep is too many. Later, zator!"

Look! Yelfred and Q-B are new best frints!

On Boborp, frints are good at sharing yunch.

But not so good at sharing frints.

Look! Some other stroodents have shared their yunch.

Omek helps Yelfred and Q-B share back!

Everyone is sharing!
How thoughtful.

Yunch ladies on Boborp do not think
so much sharing is a good idea.

Some stroodents need
to spend time by the Quiet Wall

so they can think hard about what they've done.

This is what Omek, Yelfred, and Q-B are thinking:
"I'm hungry."

"You guys want to come to my howst after skrool for some spewd?"

"Then we can play eye ball in the peedle pit!"

On Boborp, what makes things the most fun . . .

is a best frint and a *best* best frint.

"Bad frow,
you go get it!"

(Just like here on planet Earth.)

# How to count to ten on Boborp